# CONTENTS

Introduction
6

Chapter One
**Supernova Origins**
9

Chapter Two
**Stellar Creation and Destruction**
17

Chapter Three
**Stellar Variety**
25

Chapter Four
**Cosmic Influence**
33

Chapter Five
**Peering into the Universe**
41

Chapter Six
**Remnant Core**
49

Chapter Seven
**Celestial Expansion**
57

Chapter Eight
**Luminous Horizon**
62

Chapter Notes 67
Glossary 75
Further Reading 77
Index 79

# INTRODUCTION

**B**rilliant light emanating from a distant, unidentified cosmic source inexplicably appeared in an image taken during the summer night of February 23, 1987. Eighty-two hundred feet (2,500 meters) high in the southern Atacama Desert of Chile, Canadian astronomer Ian Shelton was analyzing the Milky Way's closest galactic neighbor, the Large Magellanic Cloud, at the Las Campanas Observatory. While inspecting the galaxy, he noticed a peculiar bright source of light that he could not account for.

The source of Shelton's discovery would eventually be identified as the remnants of a stellar explosion that erupted 168,000 years ago; it was the closest exploding star observed in the past four hundred years.[1] The astronomical community would soon name this stellar eruption Supernova 1987A, one of the most referenced supernovas to date.

A supernova event indicates the recent death of a star slightly more massive than our sun. During each occurrence, the matter contained within the outer layers of a star is brilliantly ejected into space. And for the most massive stars that trigger supernovas, light from these events can briefly outshine entire galaxies!

The source of these extremely luminous events primarily stems from nuclear reactions, which are interactions that occur between the nuclei of multiple atoms within the core of massive stars. Specifically, in the core, the most common elements in

# SUPERNOVAS EXPLAINED

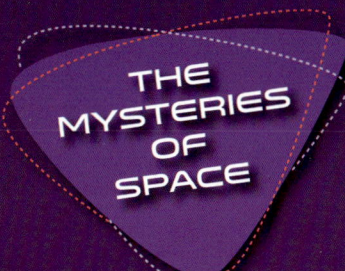

THE MYSTERIES OF SPACE

# SUPERNOVAS EXPLAINED

JAMES NEGUS

Enslow Publishing
101 W. 23rd Street
Suite 240
New York, NY 10011
USA

enslow.com

Published in 2019 by Enslow Publishing, LLC.
101 W. 23rd Street, Suite 240, New York, NY 10011

Copyright © 2019 by Enslow Publishing, LLC

All rights reserved.

No part of this book may be reproduced by any means without the written permission of the publisher.

### Library of Congress Cataloging-in-Publication Data

Names: Negus, James, author.
Title: Supernovas explained / James Negus.
Description: New York : Enslow Publishing, [2019] | Series: The mysteries of space | Audience: Grades 7 to 12. | Includes bibliographical references and index.
Identifiers: LCCN 2018016634| ISBN 9781978504585 (library bound) | ISBN 9781978505599 (pbk.)
Subjects: LCSH: Supernovae—Juvenile literature. | Stars—Evolution—Juvenile literature. | Cosmology—Juvenile literature.
Classification: LCC QB843.S95 N44 2018 | DDC 523.8/4465—dc23
LC record available at https://lccn.loc.gov/2018016634

Printed in the United States of America

**To Our Readers:** We have done our best to make sure all websites in this book were active and appropriate when we went to press. However, the author and the publisher have no control over and assume no liability for the material available on those websites or on any websites they may link to. Any comments or suggestions can be sent by email to customerservice@enslow.com.

**Photo Credits:** Cover Festa/Shutterstock.com; p. 5 d1sk/Shutterstock.com; p. 7 Celestial Image Co./Science Photo Library/Getty Images; p. 10 Mansell/The LIFE Picture Collection/Getty Images; p. 12 Print Collector/Hulton Archive/Getty Images; p. 15 Bettmann/Getty Images; p. 19 K.Muller/Moment/Getty Images; p. 20 julie deshaies/Shutterstock.com; p. 26 Mopic/Shutterstock.com; p. 28 Designua/Shutterstock.com; p. 31 Fahad Sulehria/Stocktrek Images/Science Source; p. 34 sciencepics/Shutterstock.com; p. 36 yaruna/Shutterstock.com; p. 39 AFP/Getty Images; p. 42 Peter Hermes Furian/Shutterstock.com; p. 47 The Asahi Shimbun/Getty Images; p. 50 Science Photo Library/NASA/ESA/STSCI/J.Hester & A.Loll, ASU/Brand X Pictures/Getty Images; p. 53 Mark Garlick/Science Photo Library/Getty Images; p. 55 Catmando/Shutterstock.com; p. 58 John Chumack/Science Source; p. 65 QAI Publishing/Universal Images Group/Getty Images; back cover and interior pages sdecoret/Shutterstock.com (Earth's atmosphere from space), clearviewstock/Shutterstock.com (space and stars).

INTRODUCTION

Supernova 1987A (*lower right*) resides within the Large Magellanic Cloud, a small galaxy nearly 170,000 light-years from the Milky Way. The supernova became visible in 1987 and was the closest observed supernova since 1604.

the universe, such as hydrogen and helium, are compressed together due to the gravitational forces of a star. As these elements combine, or fuse, heavier elements are produced and excess energy is generated in the process. This energy is then emitted outward from the stellar core and plays an essential role in ensuring the stable nature of a star. Particularly, the outward energy counteracts the inward gravitational force of the star to create what astronomers term hydrostatic equilibrium.

# SUPERNOVAS EXPLAINED

However, as a star ages and continues to fuse heavier elements, a threshold is met where no further combination of elements can occur. At this stage, the gravitational forces acting on the star can no longer be balanced with the outward energy generated from the fusion of elements. As a result, the core collapses in on itself. The matter within the star then contracts inward before bouncing off the core and ejecting out into space, leaving behind a dense stellar core. Depending on the mass of this core, several fascinating creations, such as neutron stars or stellar black holes, may be formed.

Comparatively, when two stars orbit one another, and one is an extremely dense white dwarf star, which is the remnant core from a low mass star that has already reached the end of its lifetime, a supernova event can also occur. Particularly, matter can accumulate on the white dwarf from the companion star and trigger the event.[2]

In general, supernova events are typically perceived as being destructive in nature, considering how most of the contents of a star are intensely spewed into the cosmos during the process. However, these cosmic explosions serve a vital role for creation in the universe; from these powerful eruptions, the raw ingredients for life and all naturally occurring elements known are produced and scattered throughout the deepest pockets of space.

These powerful explosions that occur throughout the universe serve as primary observational targets for astronomers across the globe. With the aid of the Hubble Space Telescope and the Chandra X-ray Observatory, two of the most advanced instruments utilized to study supernovas, scientists are being equipped to fully analyze these astonishing stellar bursts with the hope that further insight into their role within the universe will be understood.[3]

# Chapter One

# Supernova Origins

The study of the cosmos dates back to the world's earliest civilizations. This is chiefly because one can engage in astronomy with only the naked eye. As a result, it is unsurprisingly one of the oldest natural sciences in human history. Among the earliest civilizations, the ancient Indians, Greeks, Babylonians, Chinese, Egyptians, and Mayans actively participated in studying the motion of celestial objects in the night sky.

## The First Supernova Observations

Amid the multitude of astronomical objects visible to ancient astronomers without a telescope, from bright planets reflecting the sun's light to Earth's luminous and cratered moon, the distant stars held a particular importance. Specifically, knowledge of where the stars rose and set in the sky, as well as their motions throughout the seasons, provided a valuable source

# SUPERNOVAS EXPLAINED

Civilizations throughout history have grouped the stars into constellations. This image of a man holding a serpent, representing the constellations Ophiuchus and Serpens, is from *The Book of Fixed Stars*, a fifteenth-century work by Persian astronomer Abd al-Rahman al-Sufi.

of navigation for ancient civilizations. Additionally, by grouping stars into unique groups known as constellations, the motions of the planets and the position of the sun throughout time could be determined. In fact, the stars were deemed so relevant that extensive catalogues of these objects were developed as early as 1534 BCE by ancient Egyptian astronomers.[1]

Moreover, as time progressed, the night sky was analyzed more frequently and unique features of the stars were more closely inspected. For example, in 185 CE, an observer in China gazed up and noticed a new bright object in the sky that had not appeared before. The source of the light twinkled, but it did not move rapidly across the sky, so it was assumed it could not be a comet. The "guest star," as the Chinese astronomers called it, continued to be visible evening after evening. However, on the eighth month of observation, the source disappeared![2] What the Chinese astronomers had witnessed was the explosive death of a star, and the event, SN 185, was in fact the first ever recorded supernova.

After the discovery of SN 185, astronomers progressively recorded their observations with more precision and keenly noted instances when points of light would appear or disappear from patches in the night sky. These persistent examinations culminated in 1006 CE, with the detection of SN 1006, the brightest observed stellar event recorded in human history. For reference, this supernova appeared several times brighter than Venus, the brightest astronomical object visible from Earth, other than the moon. Astronomers in China, Japan, Europe, and the Arab world collectively confirmed the astonishing event.[3]

## **The Universe Is Not Immutable**

During the sixteenth century, the common belief in Europe was that the world beyond the moon and planets was immutable, or unchanging, as proposed by Aristotle in 350 BCE. It was then reasoned that supernovas that had previously been observed must have been an effect of Earth's atmosphere. However, in 1572, Danish astronomer Tycho Brahe (1546–1601) contested this notion. Brahe, a meticulous astronomer, performed observations of SN 1572, a luminous supernova discovered in 1572 that was visible with the naked

# SUPERNOVAS EXPLAINED

Considered to be the best pre-telescope observer, Tycho Brahe made the most accurate celestial observations of his time. Through his precise measurements of supernovas, he contradicted the prevailing notion that the heavens were fixed and unchanging.

eye. The supernova was so bright it outshone Jupiter and remained visible for nearly two years.

The thorough analysis by Brahe revealed that the supernova remained stationary with subsequent nightly observations. Consider, if the stellar explosion was within the distance of the moon and the planets, as many during the time believed, then one would expect the position of the object to vary significantly over time. For example, envision a flashlight that is illuminated at night and placed directly ahead at a distance of approximately 20 feet (6 meters) away, which is roughly the length of about ten footsteps. Ponder how the light would appear to shift as you tilt your head or move your body off-center. Now consider a flashlight that is a mile (1.6 kilometers) away, or almost three thousand footsteps away. Imagine how moving your head or body off-center will affect how you perceive the light in this scenario. It will be more challenging to detect shifts in the position of the flashlight shining at the farther distance. Brahe considered this fact and extended its implications to determine how near or far away SN 1572 was from Earth. He argued that because the supernova did not have a noticeable shift in position as Earth completed its daily rotation cycle, that the supernova must be considerably far from Earth. This conclusion directly contradicted the formerly held belief that the world beyond the moon and the planets was unchanging. Through analyzing the supernova, Brahe provided initial evidence that our understanding of the cosmos needed to be revised.

# Supernova Events from the Seventeenth to Nineteenth Centuries

Three decades after Brahe's analysis of SN 1572, an even more astounding astronomical gem appeared to the naked eye, the discovery of SN 1604. Johannes Kepler (1571–1630), best known for his theories on planetary motion, discovered the supernova in 1604. The notable stellar explosion was so bright that it was visible during the day for over three weeks. To date, SN 1604 is the most recent supernova to be seen within the Milky Way galaxy.

Similar to Brahe's analysis of SN 1572, Kepler's examination of the supernova revealed that there was a lack of daily motion when observing the source, and he provided additional evidence that the universe was not fixed, but rather a very dynamic and active environment.

Moreover, by the mid-nineteenth century, telescopes, which were first developed for astronomical use in 1610 by Galileo Galilei (1564–1642), were refined so that they could see farther into the universe. So much so that SN 1885A (S Andromedae), the first supernova outside of the Milky Way, was able to be detected in 1885. The event was determined to originate within the Andromeda galaxy, the Milky Way's closest spiral galaxy companion. Further studies confirmed that this powerful supernova was so bright that it outshined the entire galactic center of Andromeda.

## Supernovas in the Modern Era

Progressing into the twentieth century, astronomy continued to experience significant enhancements to instrumentation to bolster naked-eye and small-scale telescopic observations. In particular, a persistent astronomer by the name of Fritz Zwicky with the California Institute of Technology began a survey of supernovas beginning in the 1930s. Zwicky decided to observe the same region of the night sky every night with one of the

Swiss astronomer Fritz Zwicky poses in front of his 18-inch Schmidt Telescope on Palomar Mountain in California, 1937.

most advanced telescopes of the time, a Schmidt telescope that he developed, which contained an 18-inch (45.7-centimeter) primary mirror that could collect light from very distant celestial objects.[4] Over time, Zwicky went on to observe millions of objects in search for those select few that got brighter over time. He was determined to detect as many supernova events as he feasibly could, and at the time of his death in 1974, Zwicky had catalogued 120 newly discovered supernovas![5]

From the first naked-eye observation of a supernova by Chinese astronomers in 185 CE to Fritz Zwicky's extensive catalog of 120 supernovas detected by 1974, the field of astronomy benefited immensely from improvements to telescopes, primarily with better lenses and bigger mirror sizes. With these advancements, more supernovas were able to be detected and more information about these explosions was gathered.

Considering supernovas have quite an observational history dating back to historical civilizations, what has been learned about the source of these events? What triggers a supernova, and do all stars experience this fate?

# Chapter Two

# Stellar Creation and Destruction

Scattered throughout the universe are dense clouds of gas and dust, which astronomers refer to as nebulas. Generally, these clouds tend to form in the regions of space between star systems within a galaxy, an area known as the interstellar medium.

## Newton's Law of Universal Gravitation

The work of the English mathematician, astronomer, and physicist Sir Isaac Newton (1642–1727) provides the groundwork to comprehend the basis for which these clouds of matter concentrate. Specifically, Newton's most renowned work, *Mathematical Principles of Natural Philosophy*, published in 1687, posits the law of universal gravitation. The law states that objects have the ability to attract other objects within the universe and that negating other forces, the strength of this attraction

17

is determined solely by the mass of the objects if they are relatively close; this attraction is termed the gravitational force and is proportional to the masses of the objects and inversely proportional to the distance between them. So if two objects are relatively close and massive, then the force that draws them closer together is strong. If one object is massive and the other is not, then the gravitational force of the larger object will gravitationally attract the lower mass object. Comparatively, if both objects are not massive, the gravitational force between them is weak.

For example, imagine placing two bowling balls at opposing ends of a trampoline and releasing them. The bowling balls will tend to travel toward the center of the trampoline and eventually collide. Now consider placing two golf balls on opposing sides of the trampoline and releasing them. Assuming the trampoline is perfectly flat, these objects will be less likely to collide. This is analogous to the mutual attraction between objects of high and low mass in space.

To note, the closer two objects are to one another, regardless of mass, the greater the gravitational force between them. For example, if the two golf balls on the trampoline were closer together when released, they would in fact be more likely to come into contact despite their lack of mass.

The referenced gravitational force is in fact also the source that binds clouds of dust and gas that form into nebulas throughout the universe. The matter that comprise these objects are the lightest and most abundant elements in the universe, hydrogen and helium, which account for 73 percent and 25 percent respectively of all ordinary matter in the cosmos.[1] Over long enough timescales, these elements begin to clump together, and as small pockets of the concentrated matter become more

STELLAR CREATION AND DESTRUCTION

The Orion Nebula, which is 1,500 light-years from Earth, is the brightest nebula in the night sky and can be viewed with the naked eye. It consists of hydrogen, helium, and other gases, which enable new stars to form here.

massive, they attract even more matter. Throughout this process, nebulas can grow in size from the diameter of the moon to more than a thousand times larger than the sun.[2]

SUPERNOVAS EXPLAINED

# UNDERSTANDING THE CHEMICAL ELEMENTS

Every atom, which is the smallest constituent unit of ordinary matter, contains a central nucleus, which is made of one or more protons and one or more neutrons. Additionally, one or more electrons orbit around the nucleus. The protons have a positive electric charge, the electrons have a negative electric charge, and

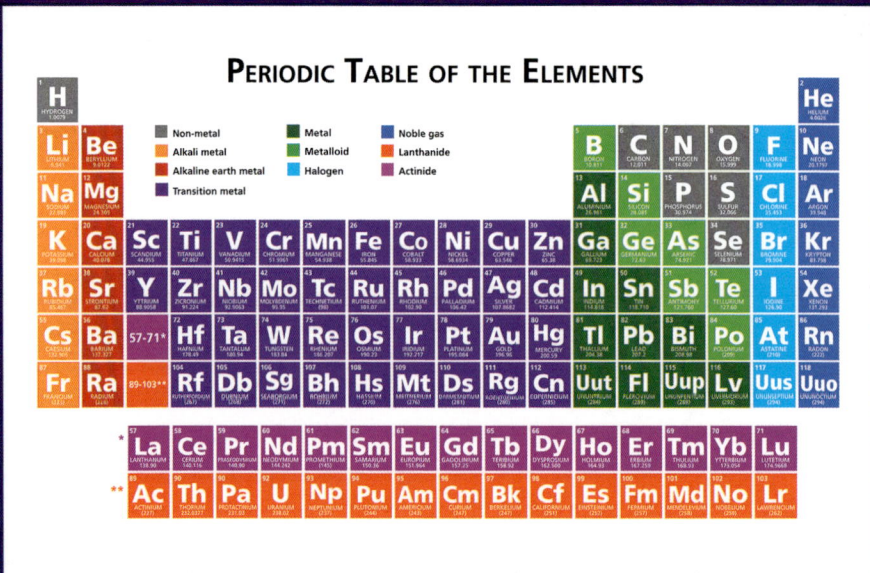

The periodic table provides an arrangement of chemical elements, ordered by their atomic number, electron configuration, and chemical properties.

the neutrons have no electric charge. If the number of protons and electrons are equal, the atom is electrically neutral; if unequal, the atom will have a positive or negative charge, and the atom is termed an ion.

An isotope is one of two or more species of atoms of a chemical element with the same number of protons and position on the periodic table but with a different number of neutrons in their nuclei.

There are 118 chemical elements; 94 occur naturally and the remaining 24 are man-made, or synthetic, elements. Additionally, the elements are numbered by their atomic number, which is the number of protons in the nucleus of an atom.

## Nuclear Fusion

As additional matter is compressed, the space between each particle is reduced. As a result, the density, or amount of mass in a given volume of space, within certain regions increases. For example, consider walking outside on a snowy day and gathering a handful of snow in both hands. Now imagine tightly compacting the snow together with both hands such that the separation between the snow particles is decreased and becomes concentrated. What is produced is a compact snowball that occupies less space than the original pile of snow. The mass of snow now occupies a much smaller three-dimensional space, which corresponds to an increase in the density of the snow. Similarly, the most common element in a nebula, hydrogen, compresses over time. In this case, rather than a physical outside force, gravitational forces are responsible for the compression. The resulting compression then forces hydrogen atoms to move faster because they have less free space to navigate. This increased motion causes regions of the cloud to heat and begin to form a spherical structure.

Eventually, areas of the nebula are so tightly packed due to the gravitational forces that hydrogen particles are forced to interact with neighboring particles. However, rather than merely colliding and being deflected, an astonishing event can occur around ten million Kelvin, which is equivalent to approximately ten million degrees Celsius or eighteen million degrees Fahrenheit, where particles actually combine and form new elements in a process known as nuclear fusion.[3] This stage indicates the impending birth of a new star.

Once enough matter is in small enough volume of a nebula and nuclear fusion initiates, hydrogen atoms begin to combine with other hydrogen atoms and can produce a heavier by-product, helium, the next heaviest element on the period table after hydrogen.

However, nuclear fusion is not a perfectly efficient process, and some energy is lost as heavier elements are created. Specifically, helium that forms through fusion is lighter than the individual hydrogen atoms that merged. The missing mass is actually converted into excess energy.[4] Additionally, as more matter condenses and fusion occurs more frequently, the combined excess energy begins to radiate, or emit energy.

Surprisingly, this outward radiation serves an extremely vital role in counteracting the constant inward force of gravity attempting to collapse the matter in on itself. Overtime, the outward energy becomes sufficient to completely balance the inward gravitational force; this state is termed hydrostatic equilibrium.[5] As a result of this equilibrium, a stable luminous sphere of gas begins to develop and form a new star.

Furthermore, once a star is formed within a nebula, it continues to grow in size and progressively fuse more hydrogen into helium. As additional energy is produced from fusion, surface temperatures can eventually increase from 3,500 Kelvin (about 3,200°C or 5,800°F) to above 40,000 Kelvin (about 40,000°C or 72,000°F).[6] These hotter temperatures cause particles to move faster and to continue interacting. Consequently, similar to hydrogen, the heavier helium matter is forced to collide with other particles within the star, which leads to additional fusion of heavier elements. Like hydrogen fusion, as helium fuses with matter to generate heavier by-products, excess energy is supplied. As the supply of each progressively heavier element is exhausted, the next stage of fusion begins to produce heavier and heavier elements over shorter spans of time.

For example, helium fusion can lead to the production of carbon and oxygen, which have atomic numbers of six and eight on the periodic table. Eventually heavier elements, such as neon (atomic number of ten), magnesium (atomic number of twelve), and silicon (atomic number of fourteen) are generated.[7]

However, for high mass stars that are greater than eight solar masses, where a solar mass represents how many times more massive a star is compared to the sun, a threshold is eventually met where heavier elements cannot be produced. Particularly, this threshold occurs once the twenty-sixth element on the periodic table, iron, forms. At this stage during a massive star's life, the iron cannot be fused to form any heavier elements due to the extremely high temperature and pressure required to do so, and thus no additional energy from fusion can be supplied.

Consequently, no outward energy is available to balance the persistent inward force of gravity.

Thus, gravity dominates as the outward energy that kept the star in balance is no longer available, and the resulting process marks the beginning of a supernova event, a brilliant stellar eruption that can outshine an entire galaxy. For massive stars, this process can occur within twenty million years.[8]

Considering nuclear fusion is so vital for stellar existence, are the processes of fusion the same for every star? How does the mass of a star play a role in determining if a supernova will occur?

# Chapter Three

# Stellar Variety

Deep within the dense nebulas that birth stars throughout the cosmos, gravitational forces bind matter tightly. Once a clump of matter approaches ten million Kelvin and an eighth of a percent of the sun's mass, nuclear fusion initiates.[1] Below this mass threshold, a smaller body cannot reach the stage of nuclear fusion and becomes what astronomers term failed stars, or brown dwarfs.

Yet, for objects that are above an eighth of a percent of the sun's mass and reach temperatures near ten million degrees Kelvin, nuclear fusion ensues.[2] Additional energy generated in the fusion process then serves to balance the gravitational forces that attempt to pull matter inward. Consequently, rather than matter collapsing in on itself, hydrostatic equilibrium is established. This condition is fundamental for the birth of a star, and as a result, nebulas with active star formation are considered stellar nurseries. However, not all stars formed within nebulas are uniform.

Consider Mercury and Jupiter, the first and the fifth closest planets from the sun. Both planets formed approximately 4.5

## SUPERNOVAS EXPLAINED

Within the protoplanetary disks that surround newly formed stars, small clumps of dense gas and dust stick together to form larger clumps. Eventually these clumps grow to become planets.

billion years ago within the same solar protoplanetary disk, which is a disk of gas and dust that surrounds a newly formed star. However, the planets differ vastly in size and mass. So much so, that approximately twenty-five thousand Mercuries could fit within Jupiter, and Mercury is nearly six thousand times less massive.[3] This type of variability among classes of celestial objects that form under similar conditions, like planets, is not unique but rather can be identified in many astronomical sources, such as stars. In fact, this variance among stars proves extremely vital in comprehending their evolution.

# The Hertzsprung-Russell (H-R) Diagram

To address the differing properties of stars, Ejnar Hertzsprung (1873–1967) and Henry Norris Russell (1877–1957) devised a system to better categorize these celestial bodies. The work they developed was formally expressed through the creation of the Hertzsprung-Russell (H-R) diagram. Within this diagram, stellar luminosity, which is the amount of light a star emits from its surface, was compared to the surface temperature of a star. In plotting this relation, they were able to showcase that stars of the same size that had higher surface temperatures tended to be more luminous.[4]

## H-R DIAGRAM DECODED

The H-R diagram was discovered independently by two astronomers, Ejnar Hertzsprung and Henry Norris Russell, in 1912. They found that when stars are plotted using the properties of temperature and luminosity, the majority form a smooth curve. These stars, of which the sun is a member, are main sequence stars.

In addition, utilizing the H-R diagram, stars were able to be better classified as a function of their surface temperatures. Specifically, stars with surface temperatures greater than 30,000 Kelvin

*(continued on the next page)*

# SUPERNOVAS EXPLAINED

*(continued from the previous page)*

(about 30,000°C or 54,000°F) down to 3,000 Kelvin (about 3,000°C or 5,000°F) were classified from hot to cold using the following letters: O, B, A, F, G, K, M. The colors associated with each star group in this range spans blue, for the hottest, to red, for the coolest.[5]

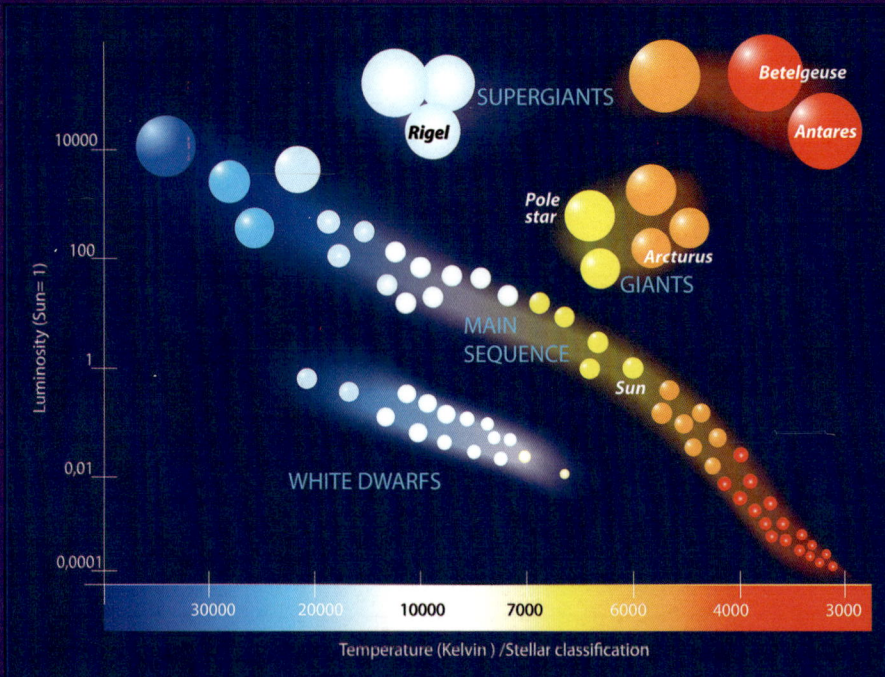

The Hertzsprung-Russell diagram is a scatter graph of stars showing the relationship between a star's brightness versus its temperature. The most prominent stars, including the sun, are along the diagonal, from the upper-left (hot and bright) to the lower-right (cooler and less bright), and are called main sequence stars. In the lower-left is where white dwarfs are found, and above the main sequence are the subgiants, giants, and supergiants.

Imagine heating two identical lightbulbs in a dark room. If the luminosity of one of the lightbulbs is adjusted so that it emits more light, the surface temperature of the more luminous bulb will be higher. This relation is one of the key features of stars that their diagram showed.

Furthermore, for varying classes of stars depicted on the H-R diagram, their evolutionary paths were shown to deviate dramatically. For instance, depending on the mass of a star, its lifetime can span a few million years for the most massive to trillions of years for the least massive.[6]

They also found the majority of stars to be main sequence stars, which nearly 90 percent of the stars in the universe are classified as, including the sun. Their mass ranges from about a tenth of a percent of the mass of the sun up to two hundred times as massive; these stars were also discovered to be powered by hydrogen fusion.[7] Yet, not all of these stars face the same fate once they exhaust their fuel.

## Death of Low Mass Stars

Specifically, for the majority of low mass stars less than eight solar masses, their cores are indeed exhausted of hydrogen. However, for these stars hydrogen fusion resumes in a shell that lines the perimeter of the core. During the process, the core of the star is converted to helium, which occurs because the mass of helium and hydrogen differ.

Consider placing two objects into a swimming pool, one being a bowling ball and the other a soccer ball. Provided the bowling ball is more massive, it will tend to sink toward the bottom, while the soccer ball will float near the surface. Similarly, in low mass stars, the density of helium will cause it to "sink" toward the core of a star, while the lighter hydrogen will rise to outer layers.

# SUPERNOVAS EXPLAINED

In this scenario, gravity continues to exert itself. This inward force results in the familiar fusion of heavier elements. Where heavier elements up to iron would be produced in higher mass stars leading to a supernova, lower mass stars lack the mass that supplies the necessary gravitational force, and resulting temperatures, to do so. Rather, fusion ceases once carbon and oxygen are formed. As with the helium core replacing the former hydrogen core, the denser elements, carbon and oxygen, now occupy the core of the star.

Furthermore, at this phase, the energy produced from the fusion process no longer balances the force of gravity, and the star is said to be out of hydrostatic equilibrium. The star then becomes unstable and the carbon and oxygen core further contracts while the hydrogen and helium continue fusion in the outer layers, which produces more carbon and oxygen that sinks toward the core. This forces the lighter outer layers to expand like a balloon, which causes the star to cool and redden; the star is said to have entered the red giant phase at this point. Over time, the star eventually becomes fully unstable and ejects its outer layer into space in a process known as a planetary nebula, which can grow as large as one light-year, or nearly 6 trillion miles (9.5 trillion km)! Left behind is the dense carbon and oxygen core.

## Death of High Mass Stars

In comparison, for massive stars greater than eight to ten solar masses, they will also reach a state where they run out of hydrogen within their cores.[8] In this case, hydrogen begins to fuse in a shell around a newly formed helium core, which causes the star to expand, cool, and redden. This stage is termed the red supergiant phase.

## STELLAR VARIETY

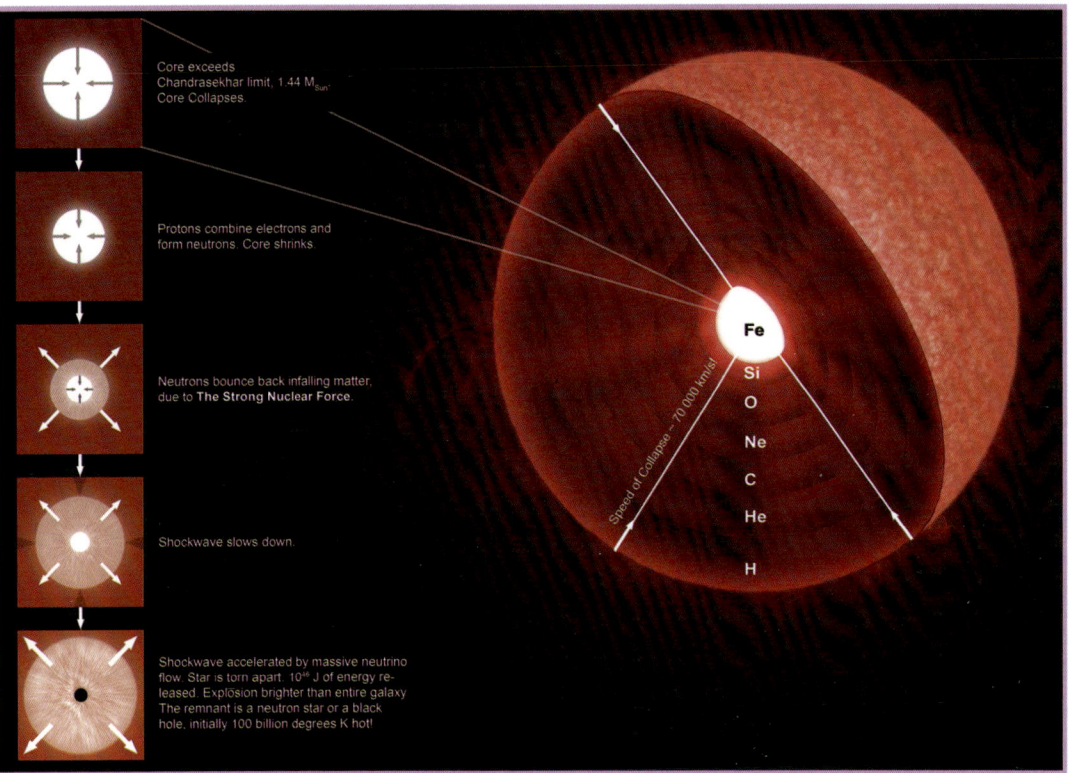

> Deep within a star, gravitational forces cause heavier and heavier elements to be formed from the fusion of lighter elements. Once iron is produced, though, no heavier elements can be generated and the core collapses due to the lack of energy from the fusion process available to counter gravity, which triggers a supernova event.

But fusion continues until iron is formed because the additional matter provides the gravitational forces and temperatures to do so. As with the carbon and oxygen core for lower mass stars, the core transitions to iron due to its high density, compared to the lighter elements that occupy the outer layers of the star.

Once this occurs, fusion can no longer proceed. Astonishingly, the star eventually begins to implode, or collapse violently inward, because gravity can no longer be opposed. In fact, the outer edges of the core collapse in at approximately 43,500 miles (70,000 km) per second, or nearly 23 percent the speed of light, the constant speed that light travels in the universe.[9] In less than a second, the in-falling material then bounces off of the extremely hot and dense iron core of the star and then back toward the surface. As the matter reaches the surface, a spectacular explosion astronomers reference as a Type II supernova is generated!

In the process, the outer layers of the star are forcefully cast into space with a tremendous amount of energy, resulting in a dazzling event so bright, that if close enough, it can be detected by the naked eye on Earth.

## Type II Supernova Classification

Additionally, astronomers have further classified these events by the amount of light emitted after the stellar eruption. Particularly, Type II-L supernovas are characterized by light that dims steadily after the event; alternatively, Type II-P supernovas radiate light and maintain constant light before falling off.[10]

The mass of individual stars serves a fundamental role in determining whether or not a supernova explosion will occur. But are there other mechanisms by which a supernova can be triggered? How can the ejection of a star's contents during a supernova event influence the surrounding cosmos?

Chapter Four

# Cosmic Influence

A Type II supernova, which occurs once iron is produced in high mass stars, is one evolutionary path that can lead to a supernova. However, there is yet another cosmic scenario that initiates these cosmic detonations. This alternate class by which a stellar explosion can occur is referenced as a Type I supernova.

## Type I Supernova

For this category of supernovas, the astronomical process of accretion becomes extremely relevant, where accretion is the process that describes a celestial body growing in size and mass by accumulating matter from a companion, such as nearby star. In the process, gravitational forces from one star tear apart layers from another, causing the host star to swell in size and mass.

In particular, for Type I supernovas, a requirement is a binary stellar system, or two stars orbiting one another. Of the stellar pair within a pre-Type I supernova binary system, one of the stars must be an extremely dense cosmic object, specifically one with a carbon and oxygen core that remains after a normal low mass star has died. These stars are termed white dwarfs.

## White Dwarfs

Understanding the necessity of having a white dwarf trigger this class of supernovas dates back to the 1920s, with the work of the renowned American astrophysicist Subrahmanyan

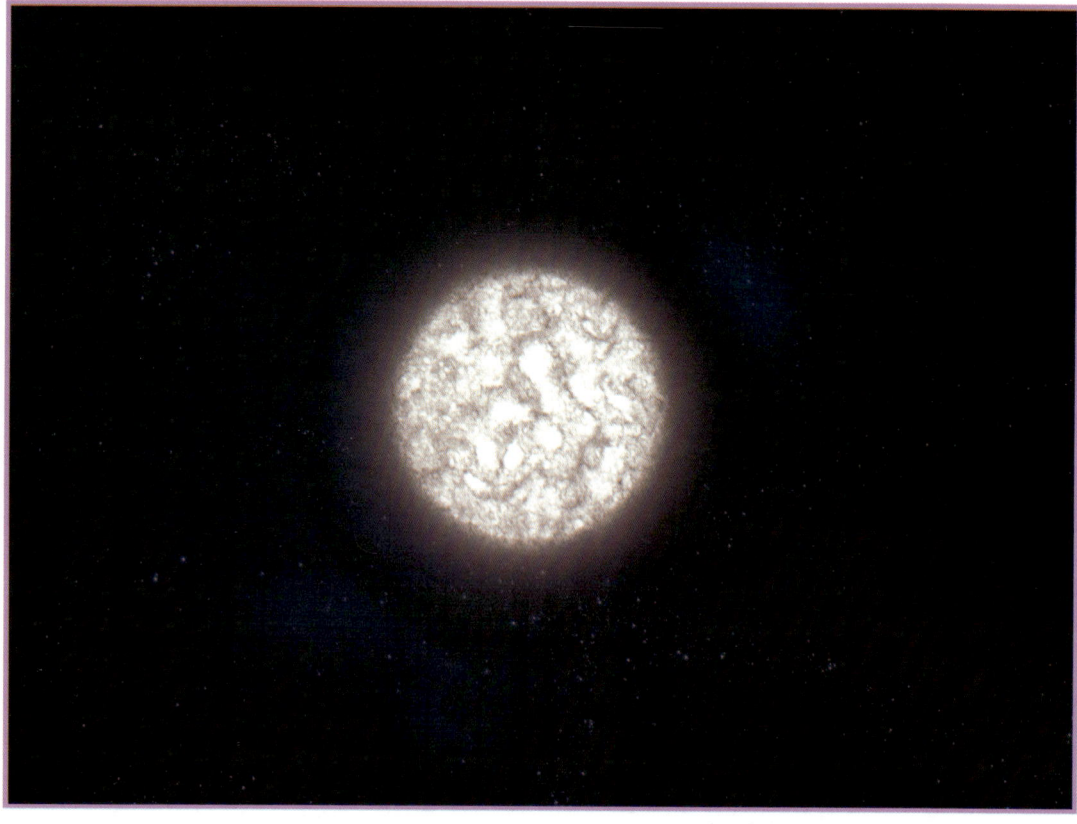

A white dwarf is the remnant core of a low mass star that has exhausted its nuclear fuel and shed its outer layers. A typical white dwarf is half as massive as the sun, yet only slightly larger than Earth.

Chandrasekhar (1910–1995) and Austrian physicist Wolfgang Pauli (1900–1958). Particularly, Chandrasekhar researched these classes of stars and noted that a white dwarf, named Sirius B, was nearly the same volume as the sun; however, Sirius B was much denser.[1] In fact, if one were to take a teaspoon of matter from Earth and one from Sirius B, the weight of the teaspoon from the white dwarf would weigh 350,000 times more.

These stars were also determined to be the remnants of stars that had already died and discontinued the fusion of elements; thus, they no longer generated the excess energy to prevent gravitational collapse.[2] However, they were still stable stars that were not collapsing. As a result, another source of outward pressure would need to be realized to account for this equilibrium.

## Degeneracy Pressure

Specifically, it was reasoned that for white dwarfs, extremely high densities result in extremely strong gravitational forces, which further compress matter within the star into an extremely small volume. Rather than fusion, though, gravity actually crushes the remains of the star to such a degree that individual atoms are destroyed. Consequently, the remaining matter consists mostly of dissociated, unrelated, individual nuclei and their former electrons.

The electrons are then forced to endure the persistent gravitational forces. Considering this fact, the solution to account for the outward pressure that ensures hydrostatic equilibrium is maintained within a white dwarf it was discovered.[3] The source of this degeneracy pressure results from the work of Pauli and the notable Pauli exclusion principle he formulated.

## SUPERNOVAS EXPLAINED

Rather than fusion, he reasoned that no two electrons could occupy the same energy level of an atom, where an energy level corresponds to a specific shell of an atom and shells further

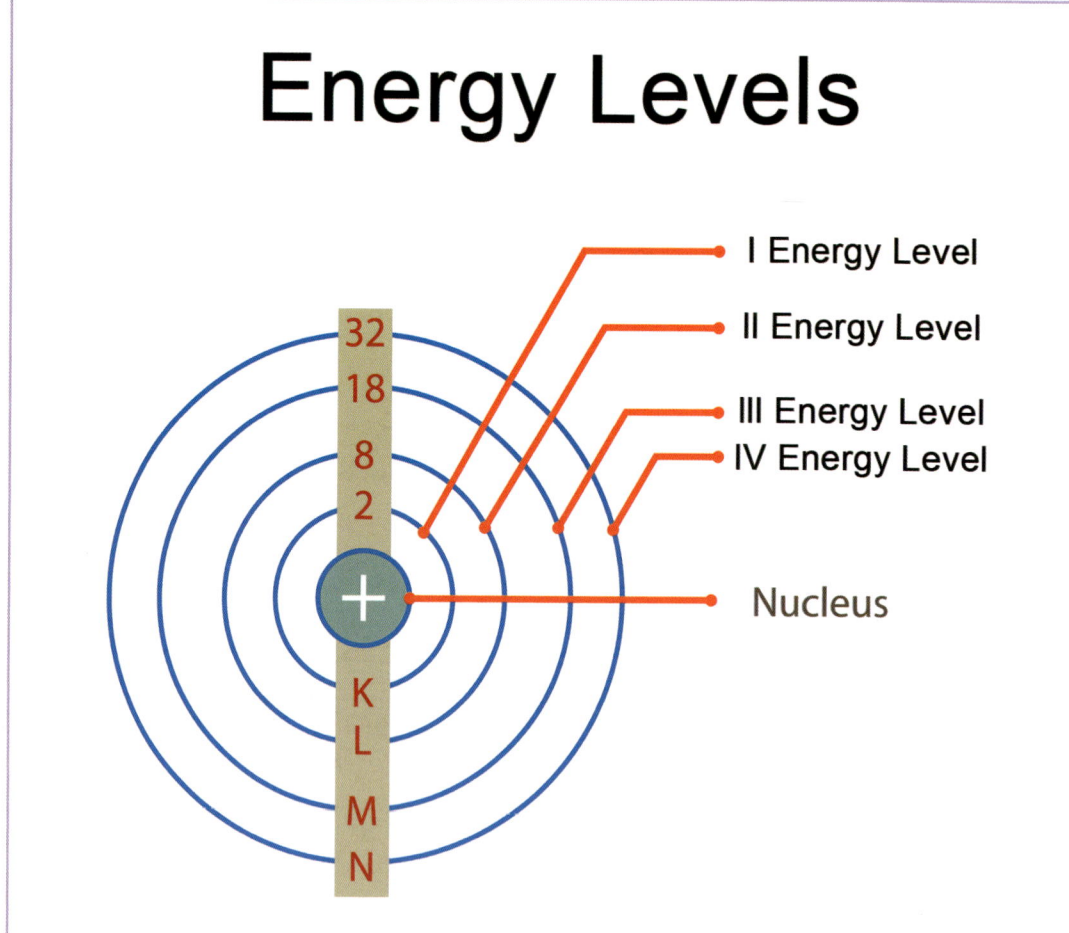

An electron shell lies outside of an atom around the atomic nucleus. It can be considered an orbit followed by electrons. The closest shell to the nucleus is the "1 shell" (or "K shell"), followed by the "2 shell" (or "L shell"), then the "3 shell" (or "M shell"), and so on. Each shell corresponds to a unique energy level and can only contain a fixed number of electrons.

out from the nucleus of an atom represent the highest energy levels. In essence, he claimed that electrons must have different energy levels, or states, and that to add electrons together in a shrinking volume, electrons must occupy higher energy levels as they cannot occupy the same level as another electron. This generated the new form of pressure, one which physicists term the electron degeneracy pressure.

Moreover, a star that experiences this pressure is said to be degenerate, and this pressure in fact proves sufficient to resist the pull of gravity for white dwarfs.[4]

# The Chandrasekhar Limit

However, even electron degeneracy pressure has its limitations up to a certain mass of the core, due the additional gravitational forces that result. Chandrasekhar would later discover this mass limit independently in 1930 and determined it to be 1.44 solar masses. This threshold would later be known as the Chandrasekhar limit, and it denotes the upper mass for which a star can no longer produce enough electron degeneracy pressure to prevent the star from collapsing in on itself.

Now to comprehend the conditions that lead to a Type I supernova, consider a binary system that may contain a white dwarf that accumulates additional matter onto it. As the mass of the star increases, it approaches the critical Chandrasekhar limit. At this critical stage, electron degeneracy can no longer resist the star from falling in on itself.

If the white dwarf core is composed of carbon and oxygen, which is the remnant core from the death of a low mass star, then it can no longer be further compressed, despite the accretion of extra matter. As a result, the core finally succumbs to gravity and collapses within a few seconds of reaching the Chandrasekhar limit.

This event leads to what is known as carbon detention, which is more commonly regarded as a Type I supernova. To note, the resulting explosion destroys the initial white dwarf, leaving no remnant, and similar to Type II supernovas, a significant amount of energy is released and an extremely luminous signature can be observed. In fact, particles in the explosion are ejected at speeds near 12,400 miles (20,000 km) per second, which is approximately 6 percent the speed of light.[5] At this rate one could travel from New York to Los Angeles in two-tenths of a second!

## Supernova Remnant

Furthermore, the outward expanding matter from a supernova explosion, for Type I and II supernovas, is termed a supernova remnant and takes the form of a shock wave, which forms when matter experiences an abrupt change of pressure and density.

Additionally, these shock waves serve an extremely vital role within the universe. In particular, heavier elements that exist in the cores of stars that undergo supernovas are ejected into space during the events. For Type II supernovas, various elements up to iron are ejected, and for Type I supernovas, various elements up to carbon and oxygen are ejected.

Amazingly, these elements alone are not the only ones that can be attributed to these eruptions. Rather, the shock waves that emanate from a dying star during a supernova produce extreme temperatures in the explosion, which serve to reinitiate the fusion process and lead to the production of elements even

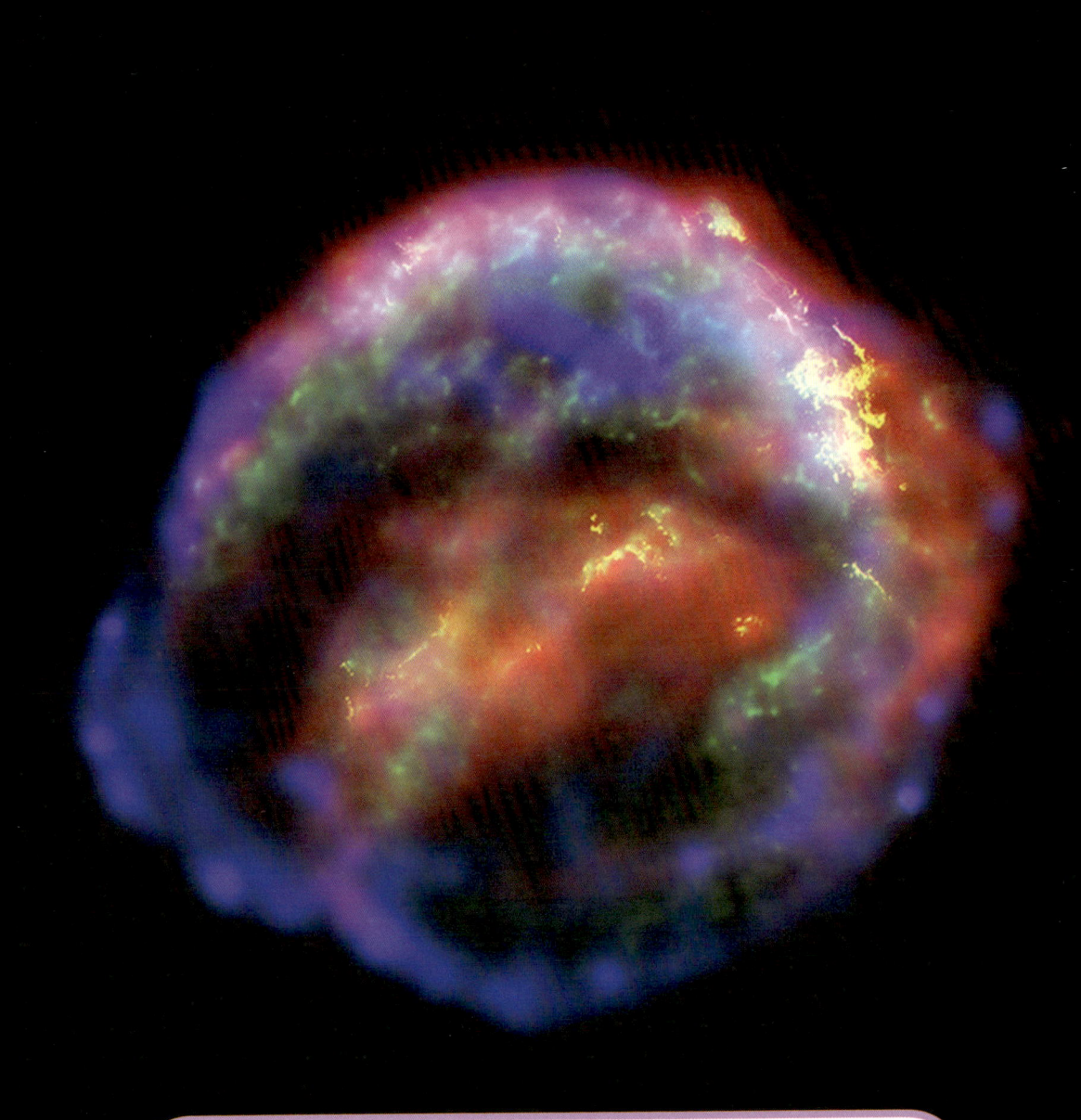

Kepler's supernova remnant is a diffuse, expanding nebula that resulted from a supernova explosion. The outer layer of gas and dust is fourteen light-years wide and is expanding at a rate of 4 million miles (6.4 million km) per hour.

heavier than iron. In fact, all naturally occurring elements that are known to date can be traced to the stars that undergo a supernova and the shock waves they produce.[6]

The types of supernova in the universe vary in how they are triggered. For some, the core collapse of a single star is sufficient. For others, accretion of mass onto a white dwarf with a carbon and oxygen core is necessary. For both, the ejection of stellar material is eventually cast into the cosmos. What, then, are the primary tools that astronomers use to study these objects? What type of insight can scientists learn about the nature of these highly energetic events through observation?

# Chapter Five

# Peering into the Universe

The first observation of a supernova occurred in 185 CE, when Chinese astronomers visually detected a bright cosmic source in the sky that lasted for several months then suddenly disappeared. During this time, the primary tool for observation was solely the human eye. However, over the millennia since this initial observation, the instruments relied upon for analysis of the cosmos have undergone vast improvements. Specifically, rather than relying upon the human eye or even telescopes, instruments have been developed to observe various wavelengths of light, which correspond to varying energies of light.

## The Electromagnetic Spectrum

For reference, light travels as a wave throughout the universe and can do so at varying wavelengths, a wavelength being the distance over which a wave repeats. For example, the distance from the peak of a wave to the next peak is a sample wavelength.

## SUPERNOVAS EXPLAINED

For light, a shorter wavelength indicates that light travels at a higher energy, and a longer wavelength indicates that light travels at a lower energy.

Consider holding a Slinky with a partner and walking away as he or she remains stationary; as expected, the Slinky will expand and the rings, which can be likened to waves, get farther apart. Comparatively, if the distance between the ends of the Slinky is reduced, it will compress. The latter scenario is analogous to high-energy light, and the former to low-energy light.

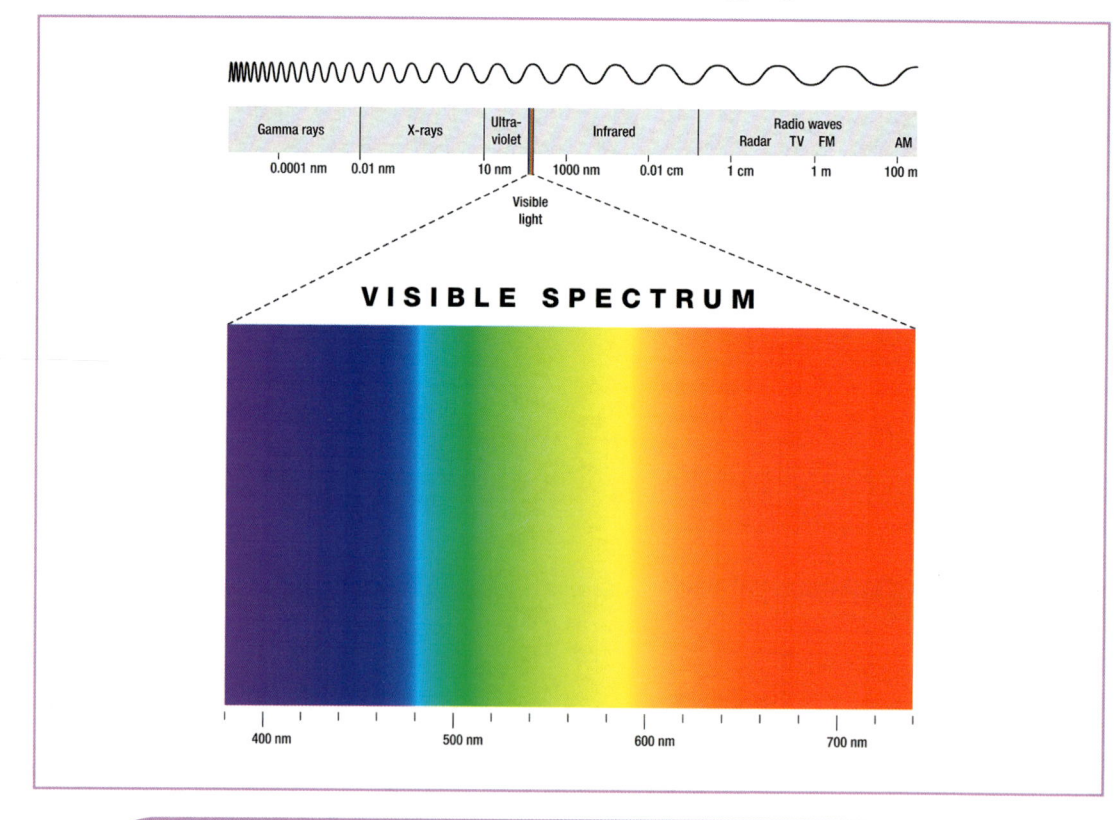

| Gamma rays | X-rays | Ultra-violet | Infrared | Radio waves (Radar, TV, FM) | AM |
|---|---|---|---|---|---|
| 0.0001 nm | 0.01 nm | 10 nm | 1000 nm  0.01 cm | 1 cm  1 m | 100 m |

**VISIBLE SPECTRUM**

400 nm — 500 nm — 600 nm — 700 nm

The range of wavelengths, or frequencies, over which electromagnetic radiation extends is shown in the electromagnetic spectrum. Human eyes are able to detect visible light, which lies between the wavelength range of 400 to 700 nanometers.

To account for the range of high and low energies that light can take, the electromagnetic spectrum was developed in 1800 by William Herschel (1738–1822).[1] In particular, the spectrum consists of gamma rays, X-rays, ultraviolet radiation, visible light, infrared radiation, microwaves, and radio waves, in order of decreasing energy. This is of relevance in astronomy because much of the light in the universe is not in the visible range but rather can only be seen at higher or lower energies.

## Swift Observatory Detects High Energies

Instruments such as NASA's Swift Observatory take advantage of this fact and are able to detect high-energy X-rays and gamma rays from space that would otherwise be unseen. Launched on November 20, 2004, Swift orbits Earth and targets high-energy events, such as supernovas, in the universe.[2] As a testament to Swift's capabilities, astronomers for the first time were able to catch a star in the very act of exploding on January 9, 2008; the star was named SN 2008D. Typically, astronomers have observed supernovas brightening days or weeks after the initial event; however, Swift was able to capture the shock waves, in X-rays, ejected from the dying star that triggered SN 2008D during its final moments of life.

## Kepler Spacecraft's Photometer

Supernovas have also been analyzed by NASA's Kepler spacecraft, a space observatory launched in 2009. On board Kepler is a photometer, an instrument that has the ability to measure the brightness of celestial objects. With Kepler, Type I supernovas have been targeted as ideal candidates for observation, primarily because these supernovas always require

# SUPERNOVAS EXPLAINED

a white dwarf with a carbon and oxygen core to be triggered at the same moment, once the Chandrasekhar limit of 1.44 solar masses is reached.[3] Consequently, astronomers often term Type I supernovas as "standard candles" because their luminosity is approximately equivalent, similar to what one would expect if a uniform group of candles were lit.

For reference, the luminosity refers to the light that is emitted from the surface of an object, while the apparent brightness is how bright it appears from a stationary point. For example, if a group of identical candles were lit on a field at night and the distance from an observer to each candle was altered, only the apparent brightness, and not the luminosity, would differ for each candle.

Similarly, considering Type I supernovas are "standard candles," they would be equally bright if they were at the same distance and differ in brightness only if their distance is changed from a fixed observation point. Astronomers rely upon well-defined equations that relate the brightness of an object to the distance to it, and thus if a Type I supernova appears brighter or dimmer, the distance to it can be determined. Fortunately, the Kepler instrument can perform the task of measuring brightness with the use of light curves, which are curves that represent the light intensity from a cosmic source over a certain amount of observation time.[4]

## Chandra X-Ray Observatory's Spectrometer

In addition to measuring light curves, instruments such as NASA's Chandra X-ray Observatory, launched in 1999, are able to identify specific elements that are generated in supernova events using an imaging spectrometer, which measures X-ray energies to uniquely identify elements.

Consider a gas being heated to high temperatures, such as with an initial supernova explosion. This process can cause electrons to jump from one energy level to a higher one. Alternatively, gas can be cooled, which can occur as a supernova shock wave expands after a supernova explosion. As the gas cools, electrons that jumped to a higher energy level when heated can fall back down to lower energy levels. In this process, they can emit light in the process. For each element, only specific transitions can occur given each element has a unique electron shell configuration; thus, unique wavelengths observed from an instrument such as Chandra can be used to identify certain elements.[5]

Furthermore, the observation of the brightest cosmic source outside our solar system, supernova remnant Cassiopeia A, was analyzed using Chandra's spectrometer. The spectrometer was able to identify unique elements while observing the remnant and confirmed iron, silicon, and hydrogen, among many other

## EXPLORING CASSIOPEIA

Cassiopeia A is a supernova remnant in the constellation of Cassiopeia. It is the brightest celestial source outside of the Milky Way galaxy. It was discovered in 1947 by radio astronomers from Cambridge, England, and was one of the first discrete radio sources to be detected. Moreover, light from the remnant is estimated to have reached Earth three hundred years ago, and its expansion shell is estimated to have a temperature around 28,000 Kelvin (about 28,000°C or 50,000°F).[6]

elements, during its observation. As a result, Chandra was able to verify that the shock wave was a Type II supernova, which is a supernova that produces elements as heavy as iron before collapsing.[7]

Analyzing the spectra of supernovas has helped astronomers in better classifying supernovas. In particular, Type I supernovas that result from the accretion of matter onto a white dwarf are termed Type Ia, Type Ib, and Type Ic supernovas, where each type is categorized by the elements that are present, or not present, in observations. For example, Type Ia supernovas are characterized by an ionized silicon signature, where ionization corresponds to an atom or molecule acquiring a negative or positive charge by gaining or losing electrons. Type Ib are characterized by having weak or no silicon absorption features in their spectrum, as well as showing helium traces. Finally, Type Ic supernovas also have weak or no silicon absorption features; however, they show weak traces or no helium at all.[8]

## Neutrino Detectors

Yet another tool used to monitor supernovas are neutrino detectors, where neutrinos are subatomic particles with a mass close to zero that rarely react with normal matter, are similar to electrons, and are believed to be emitted when a supernova occurs. In fact, researchers propose that when a massive star collapses, they radiate most of the energy that bound the star in the form of these neutrinos.

As a result, if neutrinos are emitted from the core of a star soon after it collapses, analyzing neutrino data can shed light on the earliest stages of a core collapse. In fact, the first

The Super-Kamiokande Neutrino Detection Experiment is a neutrino facility of the University of Tokyo's Institute for Cosmic Ray Research. It is located 1,000 meters (3,300 feet) underground and is designed to detect high-energy neutrinos, which are believed to be emitted from supernova explosions.

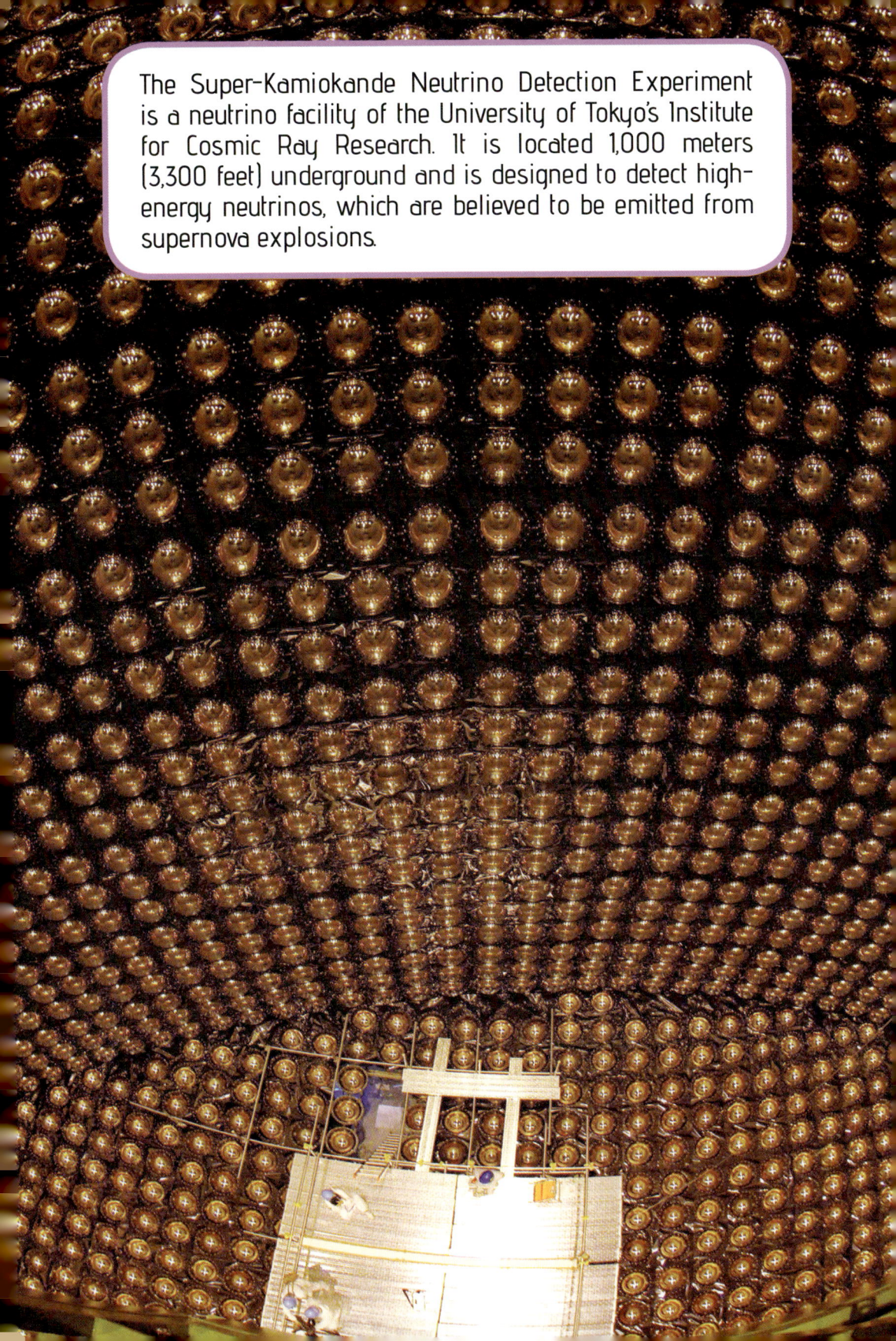

supernova to have neutrinos detected was SN 1987A, the notable supernova observed in 1987 that was the brightest observed in the four hundred years prior to its detection.[9]

## Supernova Anomaly

New detections of supernovas continue to intrigue astronomers as more unique properties of these events are discovered. For example, a team of astronomers at the University of California, Santa Barbara, and astronomers at Las Cumbres Observatory studied a star referenced as iPTF14hls. To the amazement of astronomers, the star had experienced a supernova many times over a three-year period, with an initial event detected as early as 1954. The star was referred to by astronomers as the "Zombie Star" because of its continued activity after its first death![10]

Ultimately, the tools and methods that astronomers use to study supernovas are constantly evolving. As they do, the dynamics of supernovas will be further unraveled.

But what becomes of the original star that experiences a violent supernova death? Does the core completely dissipate in the explosion or does it leave something behind?

## Chapter Six

# Remnant Core

A supernova detonation, akin to a cosmic bomb, is set off when the threshold of nuclear fusion in a massive star is met (Type II supernova) or when a carbon and oxygen core white dwarf exceeds the Chandrasekhar limit through the accumulation of matter from a companion star (Type I supernova). For each event, enough energy is generated to total the output of the sun during its entire ten-billion-year lifetime! Moreover, much of the matter from the original star is violently ejected into space as a shock wave, where it diffuses throughout the regions between stars.

In addition, the kinetic energy, which is the energy a body possesses from being in motion, of the shock waves can disturb pockets of matter within nebulas that are encountered. Specifically, the interaction can rearrange the distribution of matter in certain regions so that they clump together and ignite star formation; the addition of heavier elements delivered by the shock wave can also surround newly forming stars and serve as the basis for the development of planets.[1]

# SUPERNOVAS EXPLAINED

> The Crab Nebula is the remnant of a stellar explosion. Ejected material from the original supernova detonation expands outward throughout the interstellar medium in the form of a shock wave.

However, left behind the ejected outer layers of a star that has undergone a supernova explosion, a remnant core may exist. Specifically, for Type I supernovas, there is no remnant core left after the explosion. Yet, for Type II supernovas, there is a remnant core left after the original star experiences the event.

## Core Compression

In particular, Type II supernovas occur in massive stars that fuse lighter elements into heavier ones; hydrogen fuses into helium, helium fuses into carbon and oxygen, and this process continues until the production of iron, where gravitational forces and temperatures are not strong enough for fusion to proceed. Furthermore, as the fusion of heavier elements occurs, lighter elements transition to the outer edges of the star, where they envelop the core like outer layers of an onion. At the center lies the extremely dense iron core.

In addition, during the dramatic stellar death, nearly all of the outer layers that contain the lighter elements are shed, and in the aftermath, a dense core that no longer facilities nuclear fusion lingers. Thus, excess energy typically generated from fusion is not available to counter the ever-present force of gravity that seeks to collapse the core.

Rather, as with the white dwarfs in binary systems that precede Type I supernovas, gravity crushes individual atoms in the core out of existence, such that the remaining matter consists of dissociated, unrelated, individual nuclei and their former electrons. However, these electrons do not fuse when compressed but instead obey the familiar Pauli exclusion principle, which states that no two electrons can occupy the same energy state. As a result, electrons must occupy higher energy levels as the core contracts once lower energy levels are filled.[2] As the electrons experience this transition to higher energy levels, they begin to generate outward pressure in the form of electron degeneracy pressure, which allows the degenerate core to resist the force of gravity.[3] As with stable white dwarfs that exist prior to accumulating mass from a companion, this process is suitable below the Chandrasekhar limit of 1.44 solar masses.

# NEUTRON STAR DYNAMICS

A peculiar feature of neutron stars is that as they decrease in size, their angular momentum is conserved, which leads to the creation of an extremely fast rotating object. To envision conservation of angular momentum, imagine a figure skater spinning with arms wide open. Now as the skater draws her arms closer toward her body, the rotational velocity at which the skater rotates will increase. As the distance to the axis of rotation is reduced, rotational velocity must increase to ensure angular momentum is conserved.

If the neutron star is highly magnetized, it can also emit beams of electromagnetic radiation while it rotates and form objects termed pulsars. Most pulsars rotate just a few times per second, but some can spin hundreds of times faster.[4]

## Neutron Stars

However, for Type II supernovas, if the remnant cores exceed the critical Chandrasekhar limit, a vastly different scenario unfolds. In particular, additional mass bolsters gravitational forces and ultimately overcomes the resistance of electron degeneracy pressure.[5] Yet, considering that the core is not composed of carbon and oxygen, as with the remnant core of low mass stars, the iron core forces another series of events to unfold.

Specifically, in this scenario, the inward force of gravity causes electrons, which are negatively charged, to combine

A neutron star is formed from the remains of a massive star that has collapsed under its own gravity. These stars have very small radii and a very high density.

# SUPERNOVAS EXPLAINED

with protons in the core, which are positively charged, to form neutrons, which are particles with no charge.

Rather than further collapse, though, the newly formed neutrons in fact also obey the Pauli exclusion principle. As a result, they similarly cannot share the same energy state. To note, the differing factor in this regime is that the neutrons are able to be packed more tightly than the electrons that mostly comprise white dwarfs. Consequently, the supernova core, now composed primarily of neutrons, becomes even smaller and denser and experiences more severe gravitational compression compared to the former state of the core. This new and astonishingly dense core is now referenced as a neutron star and is so dense that a teaspoon would weigh billions of tons![6] Generally, cores between 1.44 to three solar masses experience this fate.

## Stellar Black Holes

For higher mass cores, which are greater than three solar masses and typically up to several tens of solar masses, not even neutron degeneracy pressure is available to resist the continual pressure of gravity. Consequently, once sufficiently massive, the core has no option but to finally collapse inward and evolve into one of the most intriguing astronomical objects in the universe, one that is so powerful that not even light can escape its pull.

Specifically, as the mass of the supernova core exceeds a three solar mass threshold, known as the Tolman-Oppenheimer-Volkoff limit, the core compresses into a smaller and smaller volume. As a result, its density increases as more matter from the star must fill a more compact region. Eventually, the core collapses into a region so tight that the core's matter is considered to be infinitely dense. This infinite density then creates a point in space with a

# REMNANT CORE

> The boundary in space-time where the gravitational pull of a black hole is so strong that nothing can escape is called the event horizon. It resides near the center of a black hole. Jets of charged particles, or plasma, stream out of this stellar black hole's event horizon.

gravitational influence so immensely grand that nearly all matter in its vicinity has no choice but to succumb to its attraction. In fact, a critical point is reached where the gravitational tug is so strong that not even light can escape the grasp. Unsurprisingly, this newly formed object is termed a stellar black hole.

For reference, the radius where light cannot escape a black hole's gravitational tug is known as the Schwarzschild radius, and the boundary at the edge of this radius is referred to as the event horizon. Moreover, at the center of the Schwarzschild radius is a gravitational singularity, which is a location in space where the gravitational field of an object is so concentrated that it becomes infinitely dense and the laws of physics and mathematics cease to operate. Renowned physicist Kip Thorne (1940– ) referenced the singularity as "the point where all laws of physics break down."[7]

The violent ejection of a star's outer layers during a supernova event can light up the sky like cosmic fireworks; yet, the explosion leaves behind a remnant core that can develop into a variety of objects. Depending on the mass of the remnant core, a white dwarf or neutron star can form from degeneracy pressure, or if the remnant core is too massive to resist gravity, a stellar black hole arises. Such objects are unimaginably dense, and for black holes, gravitational forces are so strong that not even light can escape.

Reconsidering the energetic shock wave that results from supernovas, what other effects could they have on the universe? Could they possibly pose a threat to life?

## Chapter Seven

# Celestial Expansion

A visually stunning supernova denotes the death of a high mass star in the cosmos. However, the majority of low mass stars below eight solar masses also experience death in a grand fashion, in the form of a planetary nebula.

## Planetary Nebula

Similar to supernovas, planetary nebulas generate an expanding shell of gas from the core of a star at the end of its lifetime. Furthermore, like a supernova, the shock wave emanating from a planetary nebula enriches the universe with elements, primarily hydrogen and helium, that promote the birth of new stars.

However, while both events similarly eject material into the cosmos, supernova shock waves are characterized by extremely high energies when compared to planetary nebulas. In particular, the hot matter that is carried away from the remnant core of a

# SUPERNOVAS EXPLAINED

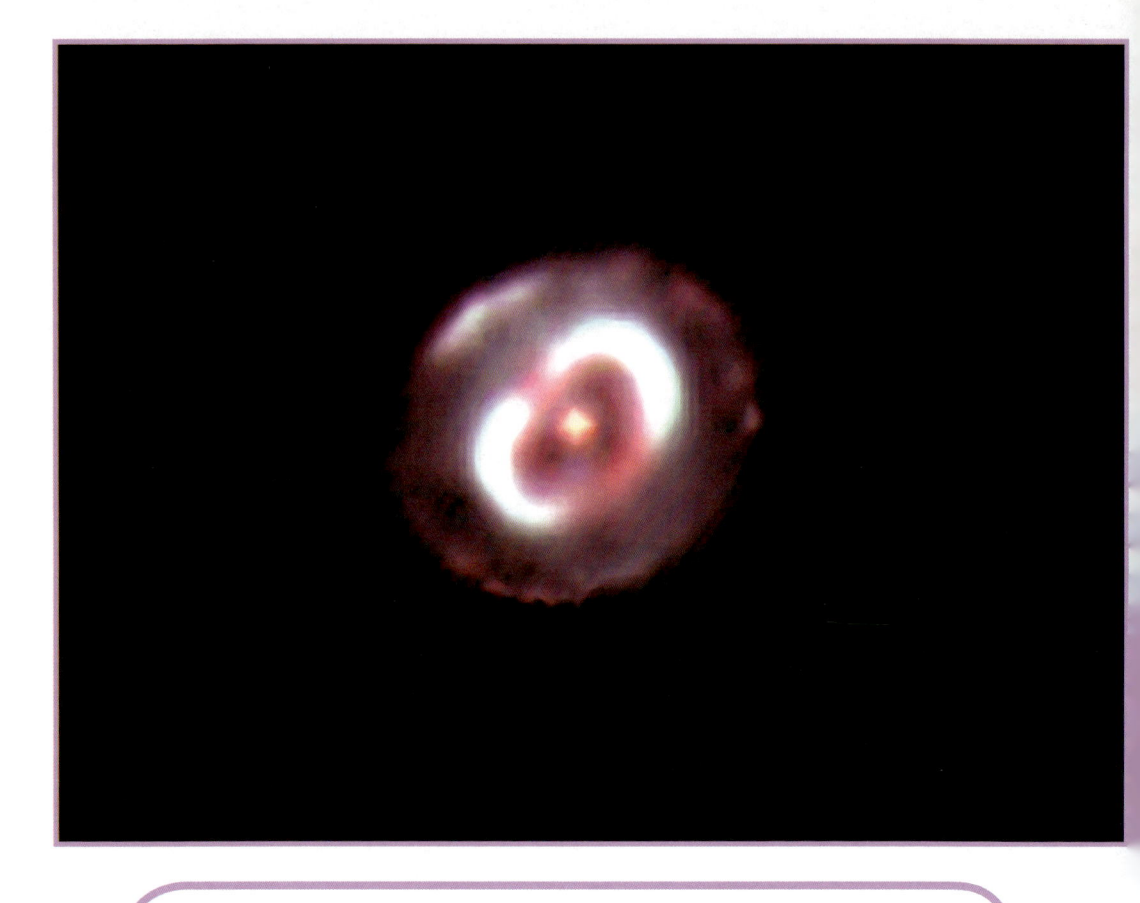

The Blue Snowball Nebula is a planetary nebula in the Andromeda constellation. The glowing shell of expanding gas signifies the recent death of a low mass star.

supernova produces X-rays, one of the most energetic forms of light.[1]

In addition, a special class of supernovas, known as hypernovas, can produce particles that are even more powerful. To note, this unique type of supernova is theorized to occur for extremely massive stars, greater than thirty solar masses.[2] The explosions they generate are cataclysmic and can produce gamma ray bursts, which are considered to be the brightest

# HYPERNOVA EVENT

A hypernova is a very energetic Type II supernova assumed to occur from an extreme core collapse. When a massive star greater than thirty solar masses collapses, it is believed to result in a hypernova, and it generates gamma ray bursts, the most energetic particles in the universe. Once the hypernova is triggered, a rotating black hole is formed that can emit twin energetic jets.[3]

Hypernovae and gamma ray bursts were definitively linked by observations made with the Very Large Telescope, operated in northern Chile, on March 29, 2003.[4]

electromagnetic events known in the universe and can shine hundreds of times brighter than a typical supernova.

## Near-Earth Supernova

Type I and Type II supernovas are estimated to be triggered only once every fifty years in the Milky Way galaxy.[5] Yet, as infrequent as these explosions may be, they can pose a severe threat to planetary bodies in their proximity.

For Earth, supernovas that occur within one thousand light-years of the planet are referred to as near-Earth supernovas. This class of supernovas can directly impact Earth, and in 2016, researchers verified that supernovas have in fact interacted with

# SUPERNOVAS EXPLAINED

Earth in the past.[6] Particularly, fossilized bacteria in sediments on the ocean floor revealed that iron-60, an isotope of iron, was present, where the isotope of an element marks a unique neutron configuration for that element.

For reference, most of the universe is iron-56, a stable nucleus made up of twenty-six protons and thirty neutrons. However, iron-60 contains thirty-four neutrons and twenty-six protons, which totals sixty. A peculiar feature of this configuration is that the additional neutrons cause iron-60 to radioactively decay, which is the process by which an unstable nucleus loses energy by emitting radiation. For each isotope that decays, the time required to decay to half of its life is termed the isotope's half-life. For iron-60, it has a half-life of 2.6 million years.[7]

Considering Earth is more than 4.5 billion years old, the presence of iron-60 suggests that it could not have existed when Earth initially formed or else it would have decayed fully by the time it was detected. Thus, it is reasoned that the source must be external. Provided supernovas are responsible for the production of the elements, specifically iron, within the universe, scientists conclude the source must be a supernova.

## The Harmful Effects of Supernovas

Supernovas can also have detrimental effects on their environments. Considering Earth, the highly energetic X-rays and gamma rays produced from these events have been theorized to have the potential to erode the protective ozone around Earth, leaving it vulnerable to the sun's rays, where the ozone layer is a protective region of Earth's atmosphere that absorbs most of the biologically harmful UV radiation from the sun. Once this layer is compromised, harmful ultraviolet rays from the sun are then able to penetrate Earth. If regions of the ozone layer are depleted, UV rays can also affect life within the ocean, where exposure to this harmful radiation can endanger plankton and reef communities, as well as the marine life they support. These effects are anticipated for near-Earth supernovas within fifty light-years of Earth; if closer than thirty light-years, the extreme radiation from the blast is theorized to potentially threaten all life on the planet as the ozone layer would be completely depleted and extreme temperatures would ensue.[8]

Furthermore, a region of particular importance near a supernova is the habitable zone around the original star. This zone refers to the area around a star for which a planet can sustain liquid water, one of the essential requirements for life. To be classified in this zone, a planet must be close enough to a star to receive enough radiation to raise water above its freezing point, but not too close that water is boiled away. This region is generally very nearby a star; for Earth, it is less than 100 million miles (161 million km) from the sun.

Thus, the effect of a supernova on a habitable planet that is near a star set to experience a supernova can be drastic. In fact, if close enough, the expanding shock wave can swallow habitable planets. In addition, planets much farther out may also be affected, as they can be flung out into interstellar space due to the highly energetic shock wave.[9] As a result, it can be challenging for astronomers to detect planets in the vicinity of massive stars that have experienced supernova events.

Ultimately, as astronomy continues to evolve, supernovas will progressively grow in relevance, for these objects may be indicators of life, or lack thereof, that can exist near massive stars outside our solar system. This is a critical aspect of why supernovas serve as key targets for scientists.

# Chapter Eight

# Luminous Horizon

The vibrant supernova remnant, or shock wave, of a supernova can be visible from a few hours, up to several months, or even years, after the initial explosion. However, the supernova remnant continues to evolve once this initial shock wave dims in a series of stages.

## Supernova Stages

The first phase of the supernova remnant is termed the free expansion phase, and it can last several hundreds of years. In this phase, the remnant has a uniform temperature and experiences a constant expansion. The second phase is referenced as the adiabatic phase, and it can last from ten thousand to twenty thousand years. During this stage, the ejected material begins to decrease in speed and mix with gas in the interstellar medium, the space between stars in a galaxy. Finally, the third phase, which is known as the radiative phase, begins after the shock wave cools down. The remnant slows down even more and begins to collapse under its own gravity. This phase can last a few hundreds of thousands of years.[1]

The length of time required for supernova remnants to evolve, as well as the time it takes massive stars to reach a supernova, make it difficult for astronomers to rely solely upon individual observations of the supernova process. Rather, they observe many stars and shock waves at varying phases in their evolution to learn about these events.

## Using Computer Models to Study the Stars

In fact, researchers take advantage of robust samples of stellar observations to use as inputs into computer simulations, where computer simulations aim to capture the behavior of a system. They are of particular importance because they incorporate several features of stars, such as their mass, size, age, and composition, to model the evolution of the stars over millions of years. In addition, researchers constantly seek to improve the inputs into their models to most accurately represent stellar evolution.[2] For example, scientists from the California Institute of Technology have created, for the first time ever, three-dimensional simulations of collapsing stars that include magnetic activity and account for general relativity, which represents the physical curvature of space as a relation to time.

## Subfields of Astronomy

In addition to stellar evolution, the study of supernovas provides insight into many other research subfields. For example, astrochemistry, which is the study of chemical substances and species occurring in stars and interstellar space, and astrobiology, which is the branch of biology that focuses on life on Earth and in space, are relied upon when considering supernova shock waves and the heavy elements carried by them, which are vital for the birth of new stars, the planets that form around them, and even life within the cosmos.

Furthermore, astronomers concerned with nebulas also find great interest in supernovas. In fact, many have relied upon observations from the Atacama Large Millimeter/Sub-millimeter Array, a series of radio telescopes in Chile, to analyze the formation of high mass stars.[3] By studying the chemical composition of molecular clouds that generate high mass stars, they can determine the key ingredients that give rise to these stars that enrich the universe with elements once they erupt in supernovas.

Yet another supernova aspect of interest is the remnant core left after a star exhausts its ability to undergo nuclear fusion. Particularly, depending on the mass of a supernova remnant core, the core can experience electron or neutron degeneracy pressure that halts further gravitational collapse. Alternatively, for the most massive remnant cores, a stellar black hole can form as the star collapses into an infinitely dense region. By analyzing the remnant cores, researchers may gain insight into the dynamics of white dwarfs, neutron stars, and stellar black holes in the universe; for example, if the frequency of supernova events in the universe can be determined, then the frequency that white dwarfs, neutron stars, and stellar black holes form may also be determined.

Another compelling case for scientists to study supernovas involves the interactions between merging companions, which are characteristic with Type I supernovas. During these events, a white dwarf accumulates matter from a companion, which triggers a supernova event. However, this accretion process is not isolated to Type I supernovas. In fact, objects such as black holes and planets can also undergo the process. As a result, insight into the accretion a white dwarf experiences before triggering a supernova can reveal the conditions necessary for these events to occur elsewhere in the cosmos.

## Continuing Observations

Moreover, as the tools for observation are improved, the depth at which supernovas can be observed will be enhanced. NASA's James Webb Space Telescope, set to launch in 2020, is the successor to the Hubble Space Telescope. It will study every phase in the history of the universe, from the first light after the big

The James Webb Space Telescope will be a able to see farther into the cosmos to image the most distant supernovas.

bang, to the evolution of our own solar system, to the dynamics of supernovas and supernova remnants.[4] Also leading the way are instruments such as NASA's NuStar (Nuclear Spectroscopic Telescope Array), the Chandra X-ray Observatory, and the Swift Observatory, which can all observe X-ray radiation from supernovas. These observations can reveal key features, such as how fast supernovas expand and how much material exists in the external shock wave.[5] These observations, coupled with faster supercomputers, will enable the most accurate models for Type I and II supernovas, as well as the cores they leave behind, to be developed.

Ultimately, there is much to learn from supernovas in our universe. They are a testament to the dynamic environments that can exist within the cosmos. Despite the violent deaths they are associated with, they play an extremely vital role. Specifically, they directly impact the formation of new stars through the shock waves of element-rich winds they cast through the ejection of a star's outer layers, and they also stimulate the formation of planets and the life that may form on them.

Supernovas are indeed one of nature's finest creations. They expose the cyclical pattern of life and death and continue to fascinate all with their cosmic brilliance.

# CHAPTER NOTES

## Introduction

1. "The Dawn of a New Era for Supernova 1987A," Hubblesite, February 24, 2017, http://hubblesite.org/news_release/news/2017-08.
2. "Type Ia Supernova," NASA, November 23, 2009, https://svs.gsfc.nasa.gov/10532.
3. "Hubble Shows Light Echo Expanding from Exploded Star," NASA, November 9, 2017, https://www.nasa.gov/image-feature/goddard/2017/hubble-shows-light-echo-expanding-from-exploded-star.

## Chapter 1.
## Supernova Origins

1. Mohammad Afiq Dzuan Bin Mohd Azhar, "The Historical Development of Star Catalogues," ResearchGate, October 7, 2015, https://www.researchgate.net/publication/282639152_the_historical_development_of_star_catalogues.
2. Sarah Zielinski, "The First Supernova," Smithsonian.com, September, 6, 2011, https://www.smithsonianmag.com/science-nature/the-first-supernova-69302940.
3. "Supernova Remnant 1006," NASA, April 17, 2013, https://www.nasa.gov/mission_pages/chandra/multimedia/tapestry.html.
4. "Decommissioned Telescopes," Palomar Observatory, updated April 18, 2016, http://www.astro.caltech.edu/palomar/about/telescopes/decommissioned.html.

5. Don York, "Zwicky Supernova Survey," ECUIP, retrieved April 27, 2018, http://ecuip.lib.uchicago.edu/multiwavelength-astronomy/optical/impact/09.html.

# Chapter 2.
# Stellar Creation and Destruction

1. "Origin of the Elements," Berkeley Lab, August 9, 2000, http://www2.lbl.gov/abc/wallchart/chapters/10/0.html.
2. John S. Mathis, s.v. "Planetary Nebula," *Encyclopaedia Britannica,* updated July 15, 2013, https://www.britannica.com/science/planetary-nebula.
3. "Stellar Nucleosynthesis," Astronomy Notes, updated June 8, 2010, http://www.astronomynotes.com/evolutn/s7.htm.
4. Chris Woodford, "Nuclear Fusion," ExplainThatStuff!, updated March 23, 2018, http://www.explainthatstuff.com/nuclear-fusion.html.
5. "Hydrostatic Equilibrium," Swinburne University of Technology, retrieved April 27, 2018, http://astronomy.swin.edu.au/cosmos/H/Hydrostatic+Equilibrium.
6. Frasier Cain, "Temperature of Stars," Universe Today, updated December 24, 2015, https://www.universetoday.com/24780/temperature-of-stars/.
7. "How Elements Are Formed," Science Learning Hub, October 22, 2009, https://www.sciencelearn.org.nz/resources/1727-how-elements-are-formed.
8. Nola Taylor Redd, "Main Sequence Stars: Definition & Life Cycle," Space.com, February 23, 2018, https://www.space.com/22437-main-sequence-stars.html.

# Chapter 3.
# Stellar Variety

1. "Stellar Fusion Requirements," University of Northern Iowa, retrieved April 27, 2018, https://sites.uni.edu/morgans/astro/course/Notes/section2/fusion.html.
2. Maria Temming, "What Is a Star?" Sky and Telescope, July 15, 2014, http://www.skyandtelescope.com/astronomy-resources/what-is-a-star/.
3. Fraser Cain, "Mercury and Jupiter," Universe Today, July 1, 2009, https://www.universetoday.com/33768/mercury-and-jupiter.
4. "The Hertzsprung-Russel Diagram," University of Nebraska-Lincoln, retrieved April 27, 2018, http://astro.unl.edu/naap/hr/hr_background3.html.
5. "Spectral Classification of Stars," University of Nebraska-Lincoln, retrieved April 27, 2018, http://astro.unl.edu/naap/hr/hr_background1.html.
6. Charles Q. Choi, "Star Facts: The Basics of Star Names and Stellar Evolution," Space.com, July 19, 2017, https://www.space.com/57-stars-formation-classification-and-constellations.html.
7. Nola Taylor Redd, "Main Sequence Stars: Definition & Life Cycle," Space.com, February 23, 2018, https://www.space.com/22437-main-sequence-stars.html.
8. Andrea Thompson, "What Is a Supernova?" Space.com, February 8, 2018, https://www.space.com/6638-supernova.html.
9. Fraser Cain, "How Quickly Does a Supernova Happen?" Universe Today, updated February 27, 2017, https://www.universetoday.com/119733/how-quickly-does-a-supernova-happen/.

10. "Type II Supernova Light Curves," Swinburne University of Technology, retrieved April 27, 2018, http://astronomy.swin.edu.au/cosmos/T/Type+II+Supernova+Light+Curves.

# Chapter 4.
## Cosmic Influence

1. "Measuring a White Dwarf Star," NASA, updated August 7, 2017, https://www.nasa.gov/multimedia/imagegallery/image_feature_468.html.
2. James Stein, "The Chandrasekhar Limit: The Threshold That Makes Life Possible," PBS, January 19, 2012, http://www.pbs.org/wgbh/nova/blogs/physics/2012/01/the-chandrasekhar-limit-the-threshold-that-makes-life-possible.
3. "Electron and Neutron Degenerate Pressure," Union College, retrieved April 27, 2018, http://minerva.union.edu/vianil/web_stuff2/Election_and_Neutron_Pressure.htm.
4. "Astronomy," University of Maryland, updated March 30, 2018, https://www.astro.umd.edu/resources/introastro/degenerate.html.
5. "Type IA Supernovae," Hubblesite, retrieved April 4, 2018, http://hubblesite.org/hubble_discoveries/dark_energy/de-type_ia_supernovae.php.
6. Dave Kornreich, "How Are Elements Heavier Than Iron Formed," Ask an Astronomer, February 15, 1999, http://curious.astro.cornell.edu/85-the-universe/supernovae/general-questions/418-how-are-elements-heavier-than-iron-formed-intermediate.

CHAPTER NOTES

# Chapter 5.
## Peering into the Universe

1. "The Electromagnetic Spectrum: A History," Spectroscopyonline.com, March 1, 2007, http://www.spectroscopyonline.com/electromagnetic-spectrum-history.
2. "Swift Overview," NASA, updated August 3, 2017, https://www.nasa.gov/mission_pages/swift/overview/index.html.
3. "NASA Spacecraft Capture Rare, Early Moments of Baby Supernovae," NASA, May 20, 2015, https://www.nasa.gov/ames/kepler/nasa-spacecraft-capture-rare-early-moments-of-baby-supernovae.
4. "Mission Overview," NASA, January 4, 2018, https://www.nasa.gov/mission_pages/kepler/overview/index.html.
5. "Emission and Absorption Spectra," Siyavula.com, retrieved April 4, 2018, https://www.siyavula.com/read/science/grade-12/optical-phenomena-and-properties-of-matter/12-optical-phenomena-and-properties-of-matter-03.
6. "Cassiopeia A," Constellation Guide, October 27, 2015, http://www.constellation-guide.com/cassiopeia-a/.
7. "X-ray Studies of Supernova Remnants: A Different View of Supernova Explosions," PNAS, February 2, 2010, http://www.pnas.org/content/107/16/7141.
8. "Type Ic Supernova," Swinburne University of Technology, retrieved April 4, 2018, http://astronomy.swin.edu.au/cosmos/T/Type+Ic+Supernova.
9. Dr. Nino Panagia, "All About SN 1987A," Hubble Heritage Project, retrieved April 27, 2018, http://heritage.stsci.edu/1999/04/sn1987anino.html.

10. Vittoria Traverso, "A Short History of the Supernova, from Ancient China to the New 'Zombie Star,'" Atlas Obscura, November 10, 2017, https://www.atlasobscura.com/articles/history-supernova-stellar-death-zombie-star.

# Chapter 6.
## Remnant Core

1. Charles Q. Choi, "Did a Supernova Give Birth to Our Solar System?" Space.com, December 28, 2016, https://www.space.com/35151-supernova-trigger-solar-system-formation.html.
2. "Spin and the Pauli Exclusion Principle," Physics of the Universe, retrieved April 4, 2018, https://www.physicsoftheuniverse.com/topics_quantum_spin.html.
3. "Electron Degeneracy Pressure," Swinburne University of Technology, retrieved April 4, 2018, http://astronomy.swin.edu.au/cosmos/E/Electron+Degeneracy+Pressure.
4. Maggie McKee, "Fast-Spinning Neutron Star Smashes Speed Limit," New Scientist, January 12, 2006, https://www.newscientist.com/article/dn8576-fast-spinning-neutron-star-smashes-speed-limit.
5. Tim Trott, "Electron Degeneracy Pressure," Perfect Astronomy, October 5, 2010, http://perfectastronomy.com/electron-degeneracy-pressure.
6. Nola Taylor Redd, "Neutron Stars: Definition & Facts," Space.com, February 23, 2018, https://www.space.com/22180-neutron-stars.html.
7. "Singularities," Physics of the Universe, retrieved April 4, 2018, https://www.physicsoftheuniverse.com/topics_blackholes_singularities.html.

CHAPTER NOTES

# Chapter 7.
# Celestial Expansion

1. "The Life Cycles of Stars: How Supernovae Are Formed," NASA, retrieved April 4, 2018, https://imagine.gsfc.nasa.gov/educators/lessons/xray_spectra/background-lifecycles.html.
2. "Hypernova," Swinburne University of Technology, retrieved April 4, 2018, http://astronomy.swin.edu.au/cosmos/H/Hypernova.
3. Ibid.
4. "Cosmological Gamma-Ray Bursts and Hypernovae Conclusively Linked," ESO, June 18, 2003, https://www.eso.org/public/usa/news/eso0318.
5. Robert Naeye, "Milky Way Supernova Rate Confirmed," Sky and Telescope, January 4, 2006, http://www.skyandtelescope.com/astronomy-news/milky-way-supernova-rate-confirmed.
6. Evan Gough, "New Estimate Puts the Supernova Killzone Within 50 Light-Years of Earth," Universe Today, May 15, 2017, https://www.universetoday.com/135534/new-estimate-puts-the-supernova-killzone-within-50-light-years-of-earth.
7. Tushna Commissariat, "Nailing the Half-Life of Iron-60," PhysicsWorld, January 30, 2015, https://physicsworld.com/a/nailing-the-half-life-of-iron-60.
8. Jolene Creighton, "What Would Happen if the Sun Went Supernova," Futurism, September 8, 2013, https://futurism.com/what-would-happen-if-the-sun-went-supernova-2.
9. "How Planets Can Survive a Supernova," National Geographic, August 5, 2011, https://news.nationalgeographic.com/news/2011/08/110805-planets-survive-supernovas-ejected-rogues-space-science.

# Chapter 8.
# Luminous Horizon

1. "Supernova Remnants," NASA, updated March 2011, https://imagine.gsfc.nasa.gov/science/objects/supernova_remnants.html.
2. Aaron Dubrow, "Supercomputer-Powered Supernova Simulations Shed Light on Distant Explosions," Phys.org, July 2, 2014, https://phys.org/news/2014-07-supercomputer-powered-supernova-simulations-distant-explosions.html.
3. "Birth of High Mass Stars and the Origin of Life," Phys.org, December 29, 2015, https://phys.org/news/2015-12-birth-high-mass-stars-life.html.
4. Brian Koberlein, "A Deeper Sky," Briankoberlein.com, May 13, 2015, https://briankoberlein.com/2015/05/13/a-deeper-sky.
5. "NuSTAR Finds New Clues to 'Chameleon Supernova,'" NASA, January 24, 2017, https://www.nasa.gov/feature/jpl/nustar-finds-new-clues-to-chameleon-supernova.

# GLOSSARY

**accretion** The gradual accumulation of matter that results in growth.

**binary system** Two astronomical bodies that orbit each other around a common center of mass.

**Chandrasekhar limit** The maximum mass a white dwarf can have and still remain stable (approximately 1.4 solar masses).

**cosmic rays** Highly energetic subatomic particles traveling through space at nearly the speed of light.

**hydrostatic equilibrium** In a star, the balance between the outward energy and the inward gravitational force.

**Kelvin** The temperature scale based on an absolute zero temperature, which is the temperature at which all molecular activity stops. Kelvin is equal to Celsius temperature + 273.15 degrees (0° C = 273.15 K).

**kinetic energy** The energy a body possesses by being in motion.

**luminosity** The amount of light a star emits from its surface.

**main sequence star** A star that when plotted using its properties of temperature and luminosity falls on the smooth curve of an H-R diagram; a star that is powered by hydrogen fusion.

**nebula** An dense interstellar cloud of gas and dust.

**neutron star** A very small but highly dense star made mostly of closely packed neutrons.

**nuclear fusion** The combination of lower mass elements into

# SUPERNOVAS EXPLAINED

**Pauli exclusion principle** The quantum mechanical principle that states that no two electrons can occupy the same energy state at the same time.

**planetary nebula** The outer layer of an old, low mass star ejected into space.

**protoplanetary disk** A rotating disk of gas and dust that surrounds a newly formed star.

**red giant** A large, cool star of high luminosity.

**spectrometer** An instrument that measures the spectra of electromagnetic radiation produced by matter.

**Tolman-Oppenheimer-Volkoff limit** The upper limit for the mass of a neutron star, which is not to exceed three solar masses.

**white dwarf** A low mass star that has used up all of its nuclear fuel.

# FURTHER READING

## Books

Binney, James. *Astrophysics: A Very Short Introduction.* Oxford, England: Oxford University Press, 2016.

English, Neil. *Space Telescopes: Capturing the Rays of the Electromagnetic Spectrum.* Cham, Switzerland: Springer International Publishing, 2017.

Gubser, Steven, and Frans Pretorius. *The Little Book of Black Holes.* Princeton, NJ: Princeton University Press, 2017.

Horn, Hugh M. Van. *Unlocking the Secrets of White Dwarf Stars.* Cham, Switzerland: Springer International Publishing, 2015.

Negus, James. *Black Holes Explained.* New York, NY: Enslow Publishing, 2018.

Tyson, Neil de Grasse, and Shelby Alinsky, ed. *StarTalk.* Washington, DC: National Geographic Children's Books, 2018.

SUPERNOVAS EXPLAINED

## Websites

**Harvard-Smithsonian Center for Astrophysics**
*www.cfa.harvard.edu/supernova/newdata/supernovae.html*
Provides an overview of the dynamics of supernovas and historical observations.

**National Geographic**
*www.nationalgeographic.com/science/space/universe/supernovae*
Discusses the importance of supernova shock waves and reviews the final states possible for the remnant core.

**Space.com**
*www.space.com/6638-supernova.html*
Offers a history of supernovas, the processes by which they are generated, and current research.

# INDEX

## A
accretion, 33, 65
Andromeda galaxy, 14
astronomy
    early history of, 9–14, 41
    subfields, 63–64
atoms, 20–21

## B
Brahe, Tycho, 11–13, 14

## C
Cassiopeia A, 45
Chandrasekhar, Subrahmanyan, 34–35, 37
Chandrasekhar limit, 37–38, 44, 49, 51, 52
Chandra X-ray Observatory, 8, 44–46, 66
chemical elements, 20–21, 38–39, 59
computer models, 63, 66

## D
degeneracy pressure, 35–37, 51, 52, 54, 56, 64

## E
electromagnetic spectrum, 43

## G
Galileo Galilei, 14
gamma rays, 43, 58–59, 60
gravitational forces, 7, 8, 18, 22, 25, 30, 31, 33, 35, 51, 56

## H
helium, 7, 18, 22, 23, 29, 30, 51, 57
Herschel, William, 43
Hertzsprung, Ejnar, 27
Hertzsprung-Russell diagram, 27–29
Hubble Space Telescope, 8, 65
hydrogen, 7, 18, 21–22, 23, 29, 30, 51, 57
hydrostatic equilibrium, 7, 22–23, 25, 30, 35
hypernovas, 58, 59

## I
interstellar medium, 17, 62

## J
James Webb Space Telescope, 65–66

## K
Kepler, Johannes, 14
Kepler spacecraft, 43–44

## L

law of universal gravitation, 17–18

## N

nebulas, 17, 18–19, 21, 22–23, 25, 49, 64
neutrino detectors, 46–48
neutron star, 8, 52–54, 56, 64
Newton, Sir Isaac, 17
nuclear fusion, 21–24, 25, 30, 31, 35, 36, 38, 49, 51, 64

## P

Pauli, Wolfgang, 35–36
Pauli exclusion principle, 35, 51, 54
photometer, 43–44
planetary nebula, 30, 57–59

## R

remnant core, 50–51, 56, 57–58, 64, 66
Russell, Henry Norris, 27

## S

shock wave, 38, 40, 43, 45, 46, 49, 57, 61, 62–63, 66
SN 185, 11, 41
SN 1006, 11
SN 1572, 11–13, 14
SN 1604, 14
SN 1885A, 14
SN 1987A, 6, 48
SN 2008D, 43

spectrometer, 44–46
stars
  categorizing, 27–28
  death of high mass, 30–32, 57
  death of low mass, 29–30, 37, 57
  formation of, 25–26
stellar black holes, 8, 54–56, 64
supernovas
  anomalies, 48
  classifying, 46
  defined, 6–8
  harmful effects of, 60–61
  near-Earth, 59–60, 61
  stages of, 62–63
  study/observation of, 11–16, 41, 43–44, 65–66

## T

Tolman-Oppenheimer-Volkoff limit, 54
Type I supernova, 33–34, 37–38, 44, 46, 49, 50, 51, 59, 64–65, 66
Type II supernova, 32, 33, 38, 46, 49, 50–51, 52, 59, 66

## W

wavelengths, 41–42
white dwarf, 8, 34–35, 37–38, 40, 44, 46, 51, 54, 56, 64, 65

## X

X-rays, 43, 44, 58, 60, 66

## Z

Zwicky, Fritz, 14–16